3/04

written by GEORGE ELLA LYON

# WEAVING THE RAINBOW

illustrated by STEPHANIE ANDERSON

A Richard Jackson Book • Atheneum Books for Young Readers
New York London Toronto Sydney Singapore

Atheneum Books for Young Readers
An imprint of Simon & Schuster Children's Publishing Division
1230 Avenue of the Americas, New York, New York 10020

Text copyright © 2004 by George Ella Lyon
Illustrations copyright © 2004 by Stephanie Anderson

Book design by Ann Bobco and Sonia Chaghatzbanian
The text of this book is set in Centaur.
The illustrations are rendered in watercolor.

Manufactured in China
First Edition
10 9 8 7 6 5 4 3 2 1
Library of Congress Cataloging-in-Publication Data
Lyon, George Ella, 1949-
Weaving the rainbow / George Ella Lyon ; illustrated by Stephanie Anderson.
p.   cm.
"A Richard Jackson Book."
Summary: An artist raises sheep, shears them, cards and spins the wool, dyes it,
and then weaves a colorful picture of the Kentucky pasture where her lambs were born.
ISBN 0-689-85169-3
[1. Weaving—Fiction. 2. Wool—Fiction. 3. Sheep—Fiction.] I. Anderson, Stephanie, ill. II. Title.
PZ7 .L9954Rai 2004
[E]—dc21   2002010717

With thanks to Dobree Adams,
whose work was the inspiration.
And for Shelby Ann Chalmers, Shelby Drew Cook,
and Gwendolyn Marie Stoddard,
new weavers—G. E. L.

For my parents—S. A.

Standing at her fence, the weaver sees
rainbow sheep grazing in her pasture.
It is spring now.
It is shearing time.

When they were born a year ago
in the dark barn
on cold March nights,
when the weaver watched their mothers
lick them clean for the first time,
their coats were white.

And they were white
when she turned them out
into April fields.

And in July
when she washed and combed them
and loaded them into the trailer
for their trip to the state fair,
they were white and bright
and they won first prize.

But they were getting closer
to the rainbow.

Fall brought their first shearing.
Then as the days turned cold
their winter wool grew in.
It kept them warm right through the snow.

Now that it's spring again
their coats are too hot
so the weaver pins each yearling
between her legs
and clips the rich wool close.
It comes off in one piece,
sheep-shape.

White and springy this fleece,
but carrying it from the pasture
the weaver sees rainbows.

She combs the wool
   free of sticks and burrs
washes out dirt and stains
cards it
   till the strands all go the same way
and spins it
   pulling and twisting a skein from the fluff
   till it's long and strong enough to weave.

When spinning is done,
the weaver draws a plan.

Then she makes her dyes
from plants she has gathered—
indigo
        goldenrod
                madder.
She is cooking up a rainbow.
In big pots she soaks the wool
like dyeing Easter eggs.

When she gets the color she wants,
she hangs the yarn to dry.

She won't be making cloth to wear.
She'll be weaving a picture,
doing with wool what a painter does with paint.

Next the weaver warps her loom.
She ties her different-colored yarn to the back beam,
then pulls it, strand by strand, to the front.
There she ties it again, making the warp.

When it's time to weave deep blue,
she'll wind that color on the shuttle
the way a painter dips her paintbrush in the paint.
Then she'll guide the shuttle
over and under the warp
to make the weft.

Finally she begins.
Feet on the treadles,
hands on the shuttle.
Back and forth, back and forth,
from the wool of her white sheep
she weaves Kentucky pastures

grass green
        evergreen
willow yellow

redbud
        purple shadow
shy sky blue

From wool looped across her hand
she weaves in lambs and their mamas.

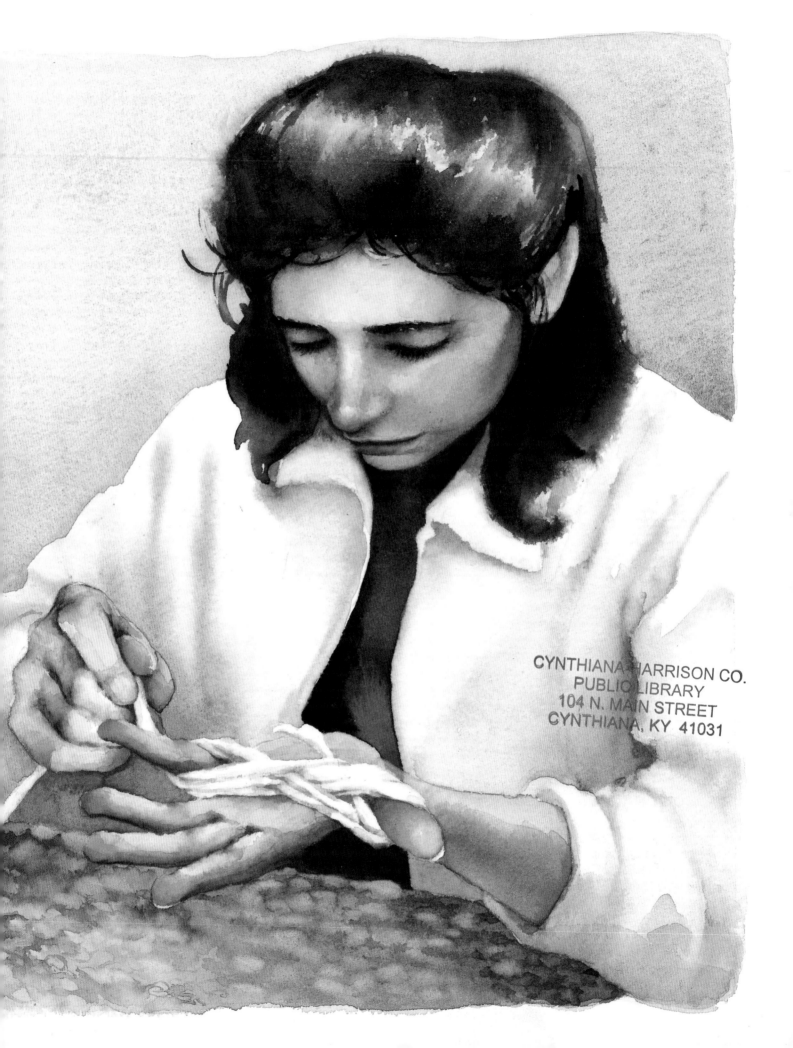

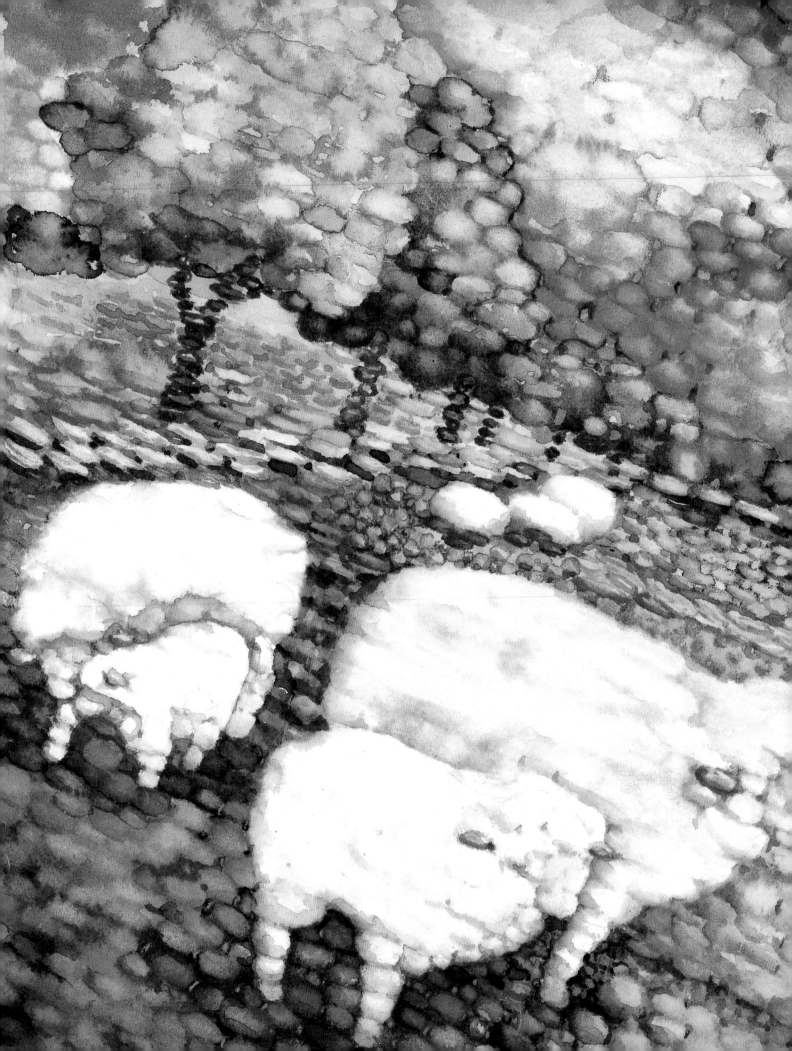

White sheep in rainbow pastures.
In rainbow pastures she weaves white sheep.